MONIQUE FELIX

THE HOUSE

AMERICAN EDUCATION PUBLISHING
Columbus, Ohio

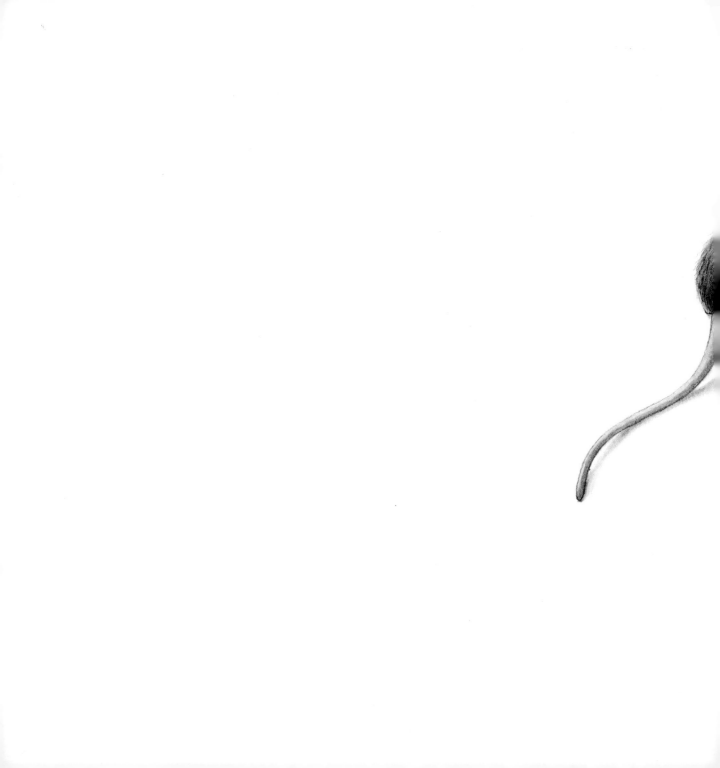

Mouse Books are designed to excite a child's imagination, develop verbal skills and foster an interest in reading. Each beautifully illustrated book allows a child to create a story while learning an important skill.

Published in 1993 by American Education Publishing

Printed in Italy.
Cover design by Rita Marshall